Bear Trouble

Bear Trouble

by
LILIAN MOORE

pictures by KURT WERTH

Whittlesey House McGraw-Hill Book Company, Inc.

NEW YORK   TORONTO   LONDON

Also by Lilian Moore
TONY THE PONY

LIBRARY OF CONGRESS CATALOG CARD NUMBER: 60–10609

PUBLISHED BY WHITTLESEY HOUSE
A DIVISION OF THE MCGRAW-HILL BOOK COMPANY, INC.

42895

For Mike

to read to Joel

Deep, deep in the green woods there was a little pond.

Tall trees grew by the pond.

Sweet grass grew all around it.

All the little woodland animals came to the pond.

They came to drink.

They came to swim.

They came to fish, or just to cool off.

Smallest Squirrel and Youngest Chipmunk
lived near the pond.

They were best friends.

They did everything together.

Once they even got spanked
together!

That was the time they woke up
Grandfather Woodchuck.

How did they wake him?

They would not tell.

But every time they thought about it,
they looked at each other—
and they laughed.

Squirrel and Chipmunk were glad
they lived near the pond.
It was a happy place.
The little animals that came
to the pond liked each other.

Sometimes the mothers and fathers
sat at the pond and talked.
If Squirrel and Chipmunk were
very, very still, they could hear
the most interesting things.

One day trouble came to the pond
in the woods.

The trouble was Big Bear.

Big Bear was getting old.

All he wanted to do now was sleep.

All day he looked and looked
for good places to sleep.

One day he came to the pond.

He looked around at the tall trees
and the sweet grass.

"How cool and green it is here!"
said Big Bear. "This is a good place
to sleep."

And it was.

Big Bear came to the pond to sleep
every day.

Soon it was the sleeping place
he liked best of all.

Now Big Bear was happy, but the woodland animals were not.

Big Bear was old, it is true.

But he *was* big.

And the little animals were afraid to go to the pond when he was there.

The trouble was that he was there all the time.

"What shall we do?" the rabbits
asked the squirrels.

"What shall we do?" the squirrels
asked the raccoons.

"What shall we do?" the raccoons
asked the woodchucks.

At last Oldest Woodchuck said,
"We must have a meeting."

So they had a meeting.

Everyone came.

Even Smallest Squirrel and
Youngest Chipmunk did not have to go
to bed early that night.

They came to the meeting, too.

"What can we do about Big Bear?"
the animals asked each other at the meeting.

They talked and talked.

They thought and thought.

"How can we make Big Bear go away from our pond?" they asked again and again.

But no one knew.

Not even Oldest Woodchuck.

Not even Oldest Raccoon.

What if Big Bear stayed on and on?

Would they have to leave this dear home by the pond?

"Perhaps," said Oldest Chipmunk.

But no one knew.

So at last they all went sadly home.

The next day Smallest Squirrel
and Youngest Chipmunk played a new game.
They had a meeting.
They sat and talked about Big Bear.
"Maybe we can scare him away!"
said the squirrel.
"Scare him away?" said Chipmunk.
"What is a big bear like that afraid of?"
"An elephant, maybe?" asked Squirrel.
"They say elephants are bigger than bears."
"Then elephants would scare us, too!"
said Chipmunk.

"Oh," said Smallest Squirrel.
"I never thought of that."

They sat and thought some more.

Then the squirrel said, "They say the old bear is BIG."

"VERY big," said the chipmunk.

"Maybe we could take a look at him," said Squirrel. "Just a little look."

"Just a peek," said Chipmunk.

So off they ran to the pond.

They did not know that Grandfather
Woodchuck saw them.

He saw them run to the pond.

"Oh, my!" said Grandfather Woodchuck.
"Oh my! They are going to the POND!

"What if Big Bear sees them?
Poor Chipmunk!
Poor Squirrel!
They are in terrible trouble!
They are in dreadful danger!
I must go for help at once."
And Grandfather Woodchuck went
for help as fast as his old legs
would take him.

Way up in a treetop by the pond,
Squirrel and Chipmunk looked down.
There was Big Bear, sound asleep
under the tree.

My, how BIG he was!

Squirrel and Chipmunk sat
very still and looked.

How VERY big!

Then something happened.

A long green caterpillar slipped
from the tree.

It fell on Big Bear.

Right on his toes.

The caterpillar began to move
over Bear's toes.

Big Bear opened one sleepy eye.

He began to giggle.

Giggle. Giggle. Giggle.

The caterpillar kept moving.

Big Bear kept giggling, "Ha! Ha! Ha!"

And he went on giggling until
the caterpillar slipped off his toes.

Then Big Bear went back to sleep.

"Old Bear is very ticklish, isn't he?"
Squirrel whispered to Chipmunk.

"Just as ticklish as Grandfather
Woodchuck!" Chipmunk whispered back.

"Remember how we woke up Grandfather
Woodchuck?" asked Squirrel.

They both began to laugh.

They both had the very same thought.

They both got busy at once.

Cut, cut, cut went Squirrel's
sharp teeth.

Cut, cut, cut went Chipmunk's
sharp teeth.

And soon Squirrel and Chipmunk
had what they wanted.

Each one had a nice long
leafy branch.

Then they began to tickle
the sleeping bear.

Tickle. Tickle.

Big Bear opened one eye.

Giggle. Giggle.

They tickled his tummy.

"Ha! Ha! Ha!" giggled Big Bear.
He tried to sit up. "Ha! Ha! Ha!"

Tickle. Tickle.

They tickled his nose.

They tickled his toes.

They tickled his tummy again.

Big Bear giggled and giggled.

"Oh, stop!" he cried. "Ha! Ha! Ha!
Oh, please stop!"

But Smallest Squirrel and Youngest
Chipmunk did not stop.

They tickled Bear's nose again.

They tickled his toes again.

At last Big Bear could not take
one more tickle.

He jumped up and ran as fast
as he could go.

He ran as far from the pond
as he could go.

"Do you think Old Bear will
ever come back?" asked Chipmunk.

"No," said Squirrel. "Somehow
I don't think he will."

They looked at each other.

"You know," said Squirrel,
"the last time we played that trick
on Grandfather Woodchuck. . . ."

"Yes," said Chipmunk. "I know.
I think we had better go right home."

Scoot. Scoot.
Scurry. Scurry.
Squirrel and Chipmunk ran down
the tree as fast as anything.

Then they started down the path
for home.

All at once they stopped.

What was that?

Was Old Bear coming back?

They ran behind a tree to hide.

Then they looked out.

What a surprise!

Not Big Bear, thank goodness!

The woodland animals were coming
down the path.

Raccoons, chipmunks, woodchucks,
squirrels—it seemed as if they
were all coming down the path to the pond
at the same time.

And Grandfather Woodchuck was
leading them.

"Dreadful danger!" he was saying.
"Terrible, terrible trouble!
    Poor Squirrel!
    Poor Chipmunk!
    Where can they be now?"

Squirrel and Chipmunk ran out from behind the tree.

"Here we are!" they cried. "Here we are!"

How surprised everyone was!

"But what about Big Bear?"
they asked. "How did you ever run away
from him?"

"Big Bear is the one who ran away,"
said Chipmunk. "Big Bear is gone!"

The animals all ran down to the pond
to see.

It was true! It was true!

Big Bear was gone!

"What made him go away?" asked Oldest Raccoon.

"We did!" said Squirrel.

"Now, now, Smallest Squirrel," said his mother. "Don't tell big stories."

"But we did," said Chipmunk.
"We tickled him away so that he will
never come back!"

"Now, now, Youngest Chipmunk," said
his mother. "Don't you tell big stories, either."

"But it is true," said Grandfather Woodchuck. "They did tickle him away. And I know how they did it!"

He looked at Squirrel and Chipmunk, and he gave them a big wink.

"It's a secret," said Grandfather Woodchuck. "Squirrel and Chipmunk and I have a secret."

He gave them another wink.

Squirrel and Chipmunk winked back.

How they loved old Grandfather Woodchuck!

That day there was a big picnic
at the little pond in the woods.

All the small animals came.

Everyone had a wonderful time.

But Squirrel and Chipmunk had
the best time of all.

They had all the nuts they could eat.

Their fathers told them they were very brave.

And their mothers gave them each a big BEAR hug!